Barbie™

HAWAIIAN HOLIDAY

First published in Great Britain 1997 by Egmont Children's Books Ltd
Michelin House, 81 Fulham Road, London SW3 6RB
BARBIE and associated trademarks are owned by and used under licence from Mattel, Inc.
Copyright © Mattel, Inc. All rights reserved.

ISBN 0 7497 3038 2
Printed and bound in Great Britain

3 5 7 9 10 8 6 4 2

Barbie and Ken's plane had just landed.
"Alan, Midge, you've come to meet us. What a surprise," said Ken.
"How was Hawaii?" asked Midge.
"Wonderful!" said Barbie.
"Come back to our place for coffee and tell us all about it," said Alan.

"Now, we want to hear all about your exotic holiday," said Alan.

"Well," said Barbie, "the day we arrived, we met up with our Hawaiian friends, Jane, Skip and Susie, on their yacht" . . .

"Welcome to paradise," said Susie.
"These garlands of flowers are to wish you
a good holiday," said Skip.
"Thank you, how kind," said Barbie.

"They smell wonderful!" said Skipper.
"I have the crown," said Ken. "So I must be the king of the holidays."

"Skip is playing the drums. Come on, let's dance, Barbie," said Susie.
"Oh, yes, I love dancing, especially the hula," said Barbie.
Skipper watched. "You're both such good dancers," she said.

Soon it was time for dinner.
"Mmm, it smells great," said Jane.
"I'm so hungry," said Skipper.
"I don't think Barbie and Susie want to stop
dancing, though," laughed Skip.

Barbie was relaxing in the sunshine the next
morning, when her friends appeared.

"Hi, Barbie. Come and play volleyball with
us," said Skipper.

"We're sure to win with you on our team,"
added Ken, smiling.

"But I haven't played volleyball for ages," laughed Barbie.
"Oh, come on, it'll be fun," said Susie.
"Well, alright," Barbie replied.

"If we win this point, we've won the game," said Ken. "Go for it, Barbie!"
"Go on, score, Barbie!" said Skipper.
"I'll try," laughed Barbie.

"Hoorah! We've won!" shouted Ken.
"What a great volley," said Skipper.
"We did it," cried Barbie. "Well done, team."

"Three cheers for Barbie, Ken and Skipper.
What a great team!" cheered Skip and Susie.

. . . "It sounds like you had a fantastic time," said Alan. "Do you have any photos?"
"Yes, here they are," replied Ken.

"Here we are with our friends," said Barbie.
"We sailed around the island on this yacht."
"It looks very luxurious," said Midge.
"It was," said Barbie. "And Skipper is still
there, lucky girl."

"This is me cooking on a barbecue," said Ken,
showing Alan and Midge another photo.
"I didn't know you could cook," joked Alan.
Ken grinned. "I'm the best!" he said.

"Here we are after the volleyball game, with the winners' cup," said Barbie.
"Oh, yes. The star players," said Midge.

"What's happening here?" asked Alan.
Barbie laughed. "We caught Jane putting
ice-cream down Susie's back," she replied.
"They kept playing tricks on each other,"
added Ken. "It was very funny."

"This looks like a market place. Did they have lots of locally-produced things for sale?" Midge asked Barbie.

"All sorts of wonderful things," said Barbie. "Exotic spices, perfume, jewellery... you'd have loved it, Midge."

"So, I just *had* to buy you some perfume," Barbie continued.

"Thank you so much," said Midge. "It smells gorgeous, so exotic."

"It was hand-made," said Barbie. "I bought some for Christie, too."

"Let's drink to Hawaii," said Ken.
"Cheers. Here's to holidays," said Barbie.
"To photos and to memories," said Midge.
"And, above all, to friends," said Alan.